Illustrated by Andrew Jimenez,
Harley Jessup, and Jason Merck

 A GOLDEN BOOK • NEW YORK

Materials and characters from the movie *Cars 2*. Copyright © 2012 Disney/Pixar. Disney/Pixar elements © Disney/Pixar, not including underlying vehicles owned by third parties; and, if applicable: Chevrolet Impala is a trademark of General Motors; Jeep® and the Jeep® grille design are registered trademarks of Chrysler LLC; FIAT is a trademark of FIAT S.p.A.; Mercury is a registered trademark of Ford Motor Company; Porsche is a trademark of Porsche; Range Rover and Land Rover are trademarks of Land Rover; Volkswagen trademarks, design patents and copyrights are used with the approval of the owner, Volkswagen AG. All rights reserved. Published in the United States by Golden Books, an imprint of Random House Children's Books, a division of Random House, Inc., 1745 Broadway, New York, NY 10019, and in Canada by Random House of Canada Limited, Toronto, in conjunction with Disney Enterprises, Inc. Golden Books, A Golden Book, A Little Golden Book, the G colophon, and the distinctive gold spine are registered trademarks of Random House, Inc.

randomhouse.com/kids   ISBN: 978-0-7364-2911-5   Printed in the United States of America

10 9 8 7 6 5 4 3 2 1

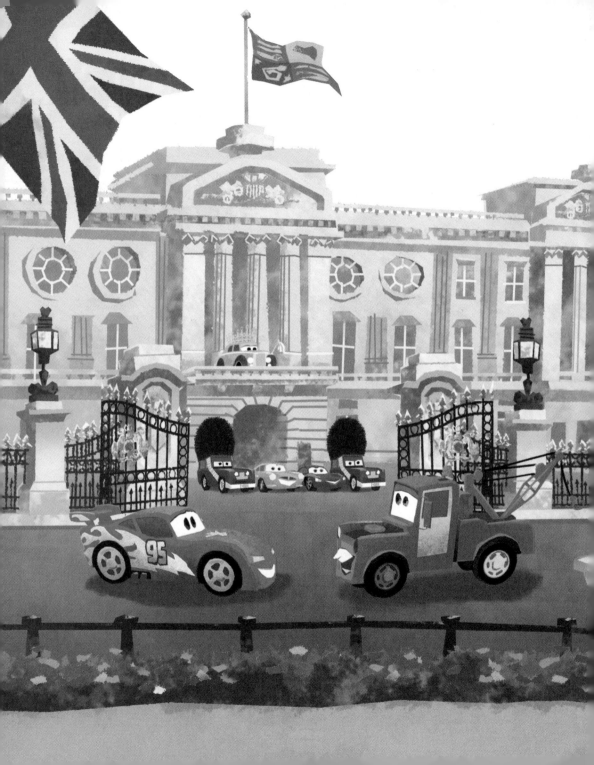

After his race in London, Lightning McQueen wanted to go home. His best buddy, Mater the tow truck, said he knew a shortcut.

"Okay!" Lightning replied. "You lead the way!"

First, Lightning and Mater went to Paris. Below the gleaming Eiffel Tower, there was something beautiful to see in every direction!

The two friends danced the
night away at the world-famous
Moteur Rouge nightclub, but soon
it was time to hit the road again.

In Switzerland, Lightning and Mater climbed a snow-covered mountain. Lightning thought the mountain looked strangely familiar. . . .

"Have you been to the Swiss Alps before?" he asked Mater.

"No," Mater replied. "But I do like to yodel—YO-DE-LAY-HEE-HOOO!"

In Spain, big yellow bulldozers chased Lightning and Mater through the narrow streets.

"Watch out!" teased Mater. "Don't let them catch you!"

"Hey, this here tower is tilted!" said Mater when he saw the famous Leaning Tower of Pisa in Italy.

Mater tugged on the tower with his tow line. But instead of standing upright, the tower ended up leaning in the opposite direction!

"Oops!" said Mater, and he and Lightning sped off.

The friends' next stop was Germany. They arrived just in time for a big outdoor party. The German cars were merrily singing and dancing.

Mater and Lightning bought matching green hats, and Mater sang along to all the German songs— even though he didn't really know the words.

"Those buildings are amazin'," Mater said as he and his buddy took in the sights of Russia.

"My face is fwozen," Lightning said, shivering from the cold.

"Well, why didn't you say so?" Mater replied.
"I know just the place where we can warm up!"

In the hot desert of Egypt, Mater posed in front of a giant statue called the Sphinx.

"Say 'pharaoh,'" Lightning said.
"Camaro!" Mater joked for the camera.

Lightning and Mater then drove along
the Great Wall in China.

"Somebody sure must have had a lot
of big tractors to fence in," Mater said.

Soon Lightning and Mater were enjoying the view of Shanghai. The city's skyline twinkled with colorful lights that lit up the night.

In Australia, Lightning and Mater climbed the beautiful Sydney Harbor Bridge. Mater loved being that high up in the air—but Lightning did not like being so far off the ground.

At a beach party in Hawaii, Mater performed a wild fire dance—until he overheated!

Before long, Lightning and Mater
were back on the mainland of America.
   "Boy, that was the longest shortcut ever,"
joked Lightning on the Golden Gate Bridge.
"But it sure is good to be home."

Finally, Lightning and Mater arrived in Radiator Springs. They told stories of their adventures from around the world.

"That trip was fun," said Lightning.

"Sure was!" Mater replied. "But next time, let's take a plane. My tires are all tired out!"